Before reading

Look at the book cover togeth title.
Ask, "What do you thin ?"

To build in not included
at the ctice, turn
back to ain with
the child.

During r

Offer plenty c praise as the child reads the story.
Listen carefully respond to events in the text.

When a **Key Word** is used for the first time, it is also shown at the bottom of the page. If the child hesitates over a word, point to the **New Key Words** box and practise reading it together. If the word is phonically decodable, you can sound out the letters and blend the sounds to read the word ("d-o-g, dog"). Praise the child for their effort, then return to the story.

Pause every few pages and ask questions to check the child's understanding of what they have read. If they begin to lose concentration, stop reading and save the page for later.

Celebrate the child's achievement and come back to the story the next day.

After reading

After reading this book, ask, "Did you enjoy the story? What did you like about it?" Encourage the child to share their opinions.

Use the comprehension questions on page 54 to check the child's understanding and recall of the text.

Ladybird

Series Consultant: Professor David Waugh
With thanks to Kulwinder Maude

LADYBIRD BOOKS

UK | USA | Canada | Ireland | Australia
India | New Zealand | South Africa

Ladybird Books is part of the Penguin Random House group of companies whose addresses can be found at global.penguinrandomhouse.com.
www.penguin.co.uk www.puffin.co.uk www.ladybird.co.uk

Penguin Random House UK

Original edition of Key Words with Peter and Jane first published by Ladybird Books Ltd 1964
Series updated 2023
This book first published 2023
001

Text copyright © Ladybird Books Ltd, 1964, 2023
Illustrations by Nuno Alexandre Vieira
Based on characters and design by Gustavo Mazali
Illustrations copyright © Ladybird Books Ltd, 2023

With thanks to Liz Pemberton for her contributions in advising on the illustrations
With thanks to Inclusive Minds for connecting us with their Inclusion Ambassador network, and in particular thanks to Guntaas Kaur Chugh for her input on the illustrations

Printed in China

The authorized representative in the EEA is Penguin Random House Ireland, Morrison Chambers, 32 Nassau Street, Dublin D02 YH68

A CIP catalogue record for this book is available from the British Library

ISBN: 978-0-241-51077-3

All correspondence to:
Ladybird Books
Penguin Random House Children's
One Embassy Gardens, 8 Viaduct Gardens, London SW11 7BW

FSC www.fsc.org
MIX
Paper from responsible sources
FSC® C018179

Key Words

with Peter and Jane

2b

Come and look

Based on the original
Key Words with Peter and Jane
reading scheme and research by William Murray

Original edition written by William Murray
This edition written by Zoë Clarke
Illustrated by Nuno Alexandre Vieira
Based on characters and design by Gustavo Mazali

Here are the shops.

New Key Words

are

FISH SH

Come and look!

Peter and Jane
are here.

New Key Words

come look

“I like books,”
Jane says.
She wants a
fun book.

New Key Words

say she want fun

"I can have a game!" Peter says.

New Key Words

can have

Peter wants a fish game.

It looks fun.

New Key Words

fish it

"Come on!"
Jane says.

She wants Peter.

New Key Words

on

Look! It is water.

It looks fun.

New Key Words

water

"Look, look! Can you look in the water?" Peter says.

New Key Words

you

They look in
the water.

They have a
fun game.

New Key Words

they

"It is you, Peter. Look! You are in the water!" Jane says.

New Key Words

"It is you in the water. Look!" Peter says.

New Key Words

"Can you jump it?" says Jane.

They can jump it!

New Key Words

jump

It is fun in the water.

Come on! Jump!

Jump, jump, jump!

New Key Words

Here is a fish shop.

They want a fish.

New Key Words

FISH SHO

They are in the fish shop.

They jump in.

New Key Words

Here are the fish.

They are here.

New Key Words

Jane wants a fish.

"Can I have a fish?" says Jane.

New Key Words

"Come on, Peter. Can you come and look? The fish are here," says Jane.

New Key Words

"I can have a fish," she says.

New Key Words

They have a fish.

New Key Words

They have a fun game.

They have a fun book.

New Key Words

Peter wants water.

"Can I have the water?" Peter says.

New Key Words

22

"I have the water.
Here you are.
You can have the
water," Jane says

New Key Words

Peter jumps on the bus.

Jane jumps on it.

Come and jump on!

New Key Words

Questions

Answer these questions about the story.

1 How do Peter and Jane have fun in the water?

2 Where does Jane get a fish?

3 What do Peter and Jane do at the end of the story?